PETER PAN

J.M. BARRIE

PLAYMORE PUBLISHERS

Editor: Heather Hammonds
Cover Illustration: Terry Riley
Illustrations: Jim Eldridge
Typesetting: Midland Typesetters

Peter Pan
First published in 2008 by
Playmore Inc., Publishers,
58 Main Street, Hackensack, N.J. 07601

Printed in China.

The Author
J.M. Barrie (1860–1937)

James Matthew Barrie was born in the town of Kirriemuir, in Scotland. He was the son of a hard-working Scottish weaver and one of ten children. He did well at school and attended the famous Edinburgh University. He then worked as a journalist, before establishing himself as a playwright and storyteller.

J.M. Barrie wrote many plays and novels. The germ of the idea for *Peter Pan* was first seen in his book, *The Little White Bird* (1902) and the inspiration for the tale came from stories that he made up for the children of some of his friends. Two years later, *Peter Pan* became a stage play by Barrie. It was a huge success. It wasn't until 1911 that the full story of Peter Pan appeared in book form.

Barrie died in London, England, in 1937. He was one of the country's most popular writers.

Contents

Chapter 1
All Children, Except One

All children, except one little mischief-maker, grow up.

Wendy discovered that when she was just two years old and playing in the garden. She had just plucked a flower and run to give it to her mother, Mrs. Darling.

She must have looked so pretty at that moment because Mrs. Darling remarked, "Oh, why can't you stay like you are forever?"

Wendy knew then that she would grow up. You always know it after you are two. Two is the beginning of the end.

The Darling family lived at No. 14. Mrs. Darling was a lovely lady. There were always lots of sweet kisses on her beautiful mouth. Yet, there was one kiss that Wendy could never quite reach.

She could see that kiss well enough. It was sitting just on the right-hand corner of Mrs. Darling's mouth. Even Mr. Darling couldn't get that kiss. And he was smarter than most.

All the boys loved Mrs. Darling when she was young. But Mr. Darling was too clever for them. While the other boys ran to her door to ask her to marry them, Mr. Darling took a taxi and nipped in first. So they were married and had three children. Wendy came first, then John, and finally Michael, the baby of the family.

With three mouths to feed, the family was quite poor. Mr. Darling did get a nurse to help with the children. But because they were so short of money, they found a kindly old dog called Nana to do the job.

Nana had spent most of her life trotting about in Kensington Gardens, one of the biggest parks in London. She just loved looking into baby carriages to make sure the occupants were happy and well. Nana was born to look after children.

And so Nana came to live with the Darlings. She proved an absolute treasure.

She had her own kennel in the nursery, and she was up in a flash if she heard any child cry in the night.

Nana liked to keep discipline though. When she walked the children to school, she expected

"Oh, why can't you stay like you are forever?"

3

them to stay in line. If they didn't, she'd affectionately push them back in again with her nose. Nana felt rather superior to the human nurses that used to bring all the other children to school.

All the family loved Nana, although Mr. Darling was never quite sure that the dog approved of him. Mr. Darling always thought that Nana should have shown him more respect. But all in all, the Darlings, the three children, and Nana lived a happy life.

In fact, there never was a happier family until the coming of Peter Pan.

Mrs. Darling first heard of Peter Pan when she was tidying up her children's minds. Every night at bedtime she would rummage through Wendy, John, and Michael's minds, putting things straight and tidying for the next morning. It was really just like tidying up the contents of a chest of drawers.

I don't know whether you have seen a map of a child's mind. But it is full of memories, love, school lessons, friends, and a place called Neverland. All children have a Neverland in their heads. It's usually an island that only they can reach. Parents never go there.

Of course, Neverlands vary a great deal.

Nana proved an absolute treasure.

John's Neverland had a lagoon with flamingoes flying over it. Michael, who was very small, had a flamingo with a lagoon flying over it.

John's home in Neverland was an upside-down boat. Michael's was a wigwam.

Wendy's Neverland home was a house of leaves sewn together. She also had a pet wolf for a friend.

Mrs. Darling often found these places when she was sorting through her children's minds. Sometimes she found things she couldn't understand, and one of the most puzzling things she found was the name Peter. Mrs. Darling knew of no Peter. Yet, there was his name, in all her children's minds.

"Who is Peter?" Mrs. Darling asked Wendy one night.

"He is Peter Pan," said Wendy. "You must know him, Mother."

Mrs. Darling thought back to her own childhood. Did she remember a Peter Pan? Didn't he live with the fairies? She decided that if she did believe in Peter Pan when she was young, then she doubted whether there was any such person now.

"If he was real," she said, "he would be very grown-up by now."

"Oh no!" cried Wendy. "He isn't a grown-up at all. He is just my size and age."

That evening, Mrs. Darling spoke to her husband about it. He said it was all nonsense that Nana had probably put into Wendy's head. "It's just the sort of idea a dog would have," he said very seriously. "It will soon blow over."

But it didn't blow over, and the troublesome boy called Peter gave Mrs. Darling quite a shock the next day.

Chapter 2
Peter Loses his Shadow

The next morning, Mrs. Darling found some leaves lying on the nursery floor.

"Where did these come from?" she asked.

"Peter Pan must have brought them in, stuck to his shoes," replied Wendy.

"What do you mean?" asked Mrs. Darling.

"I know he's been naughty," said Wendy. "He should have wiped his feet when he came in."

"What nonsense you talk, dear," said Mrs. Darling. "No one can get into the house without knocking on the front door."

"I think he comes in by the window," said Wendy.

"My love," said Mrs. Darling, "the nursery is three floors up. You must be dreaming."

But Wendy wasn't dreaming, as the very next night revealed. The children were all in bed. It happened to be Nana's night off. So Mrs. Darling had bathed them and sung to them until, one by one, they had let go of her hand and slid away to the land of sleep.

The fire was warm and the nursery was dimly lit by three night lights. Mrs. Darling, who had sat down in a chair to read for a while, started to nod off. Soon she was asleep.

While she slept, the window of the nursery blew open and a little boy dropped down onto the floor. The breeze woke Mrs. Darling and she started up with a cry when she saw the boy. Somehow, she knew at once that it was Peter Pan. He was a lovely child, dressed in an outfit of skeleton leaves. When he saw that Mrs. Darling was a grown-up, he pulled a face at her.

Mrs. Darling screamed.

Nana, who had just returned from her night out, pounded into the nursery. She growled and sprang at the boy, who leapt out of the window just before she slammed it shut.

Mrs. Darling screamed again, this time in distress. She thought the boy must have fallen down into the street below. She looked out of the window but saw nothing except a beautiful, starry sky.

Mrs. Darling turned around. Nana now had something in her mouth. It was quite clearly the boy's shadow! For a moment, Mrs. Darling didn't know what to do with it. Then she rolled it up and put it carefully in a drawer.

And there the shadow lay until the following Friday night when Mr. and Mrs. Darling were due to dine with their friends, just down the street at No. 27.

The evening began as usual, with little Michael refusing to leave his warm bath until Nana carried him to bed on her back. Before the Darlings left, they came to say goodnight to the children.

"Isn't Nana a treasure," said Mrs. Darling, seeing the dog getting the children into bed.

"She might be," replied Mr. Darling, rather seriously. "But I fear she looks on the children as puppies."

Mr. Darling had never liked dogs as much as his wife. "The proper place for a dog is in the yard," he said. "From now on, after the children are in bed, Nana must be taken out and tied in the yard."

The children cried out in protest. They loved having Nana guarding them in the nursery at night.

"No!" said Mr. Darling, firmly. "Nana must sleep outside, starting tonight."

She knew at once that it was Peter Pan.

Mr. Darling could not be persuaded otherwise and he led Nana away. When he returned to the nursery, they could all hear Nana barking outside in the yard.

"That is not Nana's unhappy bark," said Wendy. "That's the bark she makes when she smells danger."

"Are you sure, Wendy?" said Mrs. Darling.

"Oh, yes," said Wendy.

Now Mrs. Darling was worried. She went to the window to make sure it was fastened. She looked out and saw that the sky was peppered with stars. They seemed to be crowding around the house, watching and waiting.

Mrs. Darling suddenly felt frightened. "Oh I wish I wasn't going out tonight," she said.

Michael knew his mother was worried about something. "Can anything harm us," he asked, "after the night lights have been lit?"

"Of course not," said Mrs. Darling. "Night lights are the eyes a mother leaves behind to guard her children."

The Darlings kissed their children goodnight and left, shutting the door behind them. No. 27 was only a few yards away from their own house. It had been snowing and they tiptoed along so they didn't get their shoes wet.

"Nana must sleep outside."

They were the only people in the street and all
the stars were still watching and waiting.

As soon as the Darlings were inside No. 27
and the door shut, there was a commotion in
the heavens.

The smallest of the stars in the Milky Way
screamed out:

"Now Peter! Now!"

Chapter 3
Peter and Tinker Bell Fly In

Inside the nursery, Wendy, John, and Michael were fast asleep. Something moved by the window. The night-lights flickered and went out.

There was another light in the room now, a thousand times brighter than the night-lights. It darted here and there, in and out of cupboards and under the beds. It flew around the room so quickly, that it was only when it stopped for a moment that you saw what it was.

It wasn't a light at all. It was a fairy, no taller than the length of your hand. She was called Tinker Bell, and she was beautifully dressed in a gown of skeleton leaves.

A moment after her entrance, the window was blown open by the breathing of the stars and Peter dropped in.

"Tink," he called softly, "have you found my shadow yet?"

Tinker Bell answered with a voice that was

Tinker Bell darted here and there.

a lovely mix of tinkling fairy bells. "It's in the chest of drawers, I think," she said, diving into the half-opened top drawer.

Peter jumped in too, scattering the contents all over the floor. He found his shadow where Mrs. Darling had left it, but then he discovered a terrible problem. He couldn't put his shadow back on.

He went to the bathroom and tried to stick it on with soap. That didn't work. So he returned to the nursery and tried to tie it on with string. That was hopeless. At last, he gave up and sat on the floor and burst into tears.

Trying to tie his shadow on.

Peter's sobs woke Wendy, and she sat up in bed. The sight of the boy didn't frighten her at all. "Why are you crying?" she asked.

Peter could be very polite at times. He stopped crying immediately, stood up and bowed to Wendy. She was so delighted that she bowed back to Peter from her bed.

"What's your name?" he asked.

"Wendy Moira Angela Darling," she answered. "And who are you?"

"Peter Pan," he announced proudly.

"I thought you might be," she said. "Where do you live?"

"Second to the right," said Peter, "and straight on till morning."

"What a funny address," said Wendy.

"No it isn't," he replied.

"Is that the address people put on your letters?" she asked.

"I don't get letters," said Peter.

"But your mother must get letters," said Wendy.

"I don't have a mother," was the reply. "And I don't think I want one either. They are greatly overrated."

Wendy felt so sad when she heard this. "No wonder you were crying when I woke up," she said. "It must be sad not to have a mother."

"I wasn't crying about mothers," said Peter, rather rudely. "I was crying because I can't put my shadow back on. Besides, I wasn't really crying."

Wendy saw the shadow lying on the floor. Fortunately, she knew exactly what to do. "It must be sewn on," she said. "I'll sew it on for you. It might hurt a little."

"Oh, I shan't cry," said Peter, who was now quite convinced that he had never cried in his life.

So Wendy took a needle and thread from the cupboard beside her bed and sewed the shadow on. It didn't hurt either.

You would have thought Peter had sewed it on himself. "Oh, what a clever boy I am!" he crowed.

Wendy decided she had never met such a cocky boy in her life. "Of course, the sewing was nothing to do with me," she said.

"Oh, just a little," insisted Peter. "But it was mainly me."

"Then you won't need me again," she snapped.

With that, she slid down the bed and covered herself with blankets.

"Oh do come back, Wendy," cried Peter. "I can't help crowing when I'm pleased with myself."

Still Wendy wouldn't come out from under the blankets.

"Wendy," he whispered in his most gentle voice. "Please come out. I know really that girls are much more useful than boys."

"Do you really think so?" asked Wendy, peeping over the bedclothes.

"I truly do," said Peter.

"That is very sweet of you to say so," said Wendy. "I'll reward you with a kiss."

Peter held out his hand, as if waiting for Wendy to give him something.

"Surely you know what a kiss is?" said Wendy.

"I shall do when you give me one," replied Peter, obstinately.

Wendy knew then that Peter had no idea what a kiss was. So she gave him a thimble instead.

"Now I'll give you a kiss," said Peter, giving Wendy one of the buttons from her sewing kit.

Wendy thanked him and said she would wear his kiss on a chain around her neck. "How old are you, Peter?" she asked.

"Oh, what a clever boy I am!"

"I don't know," said the boy. "I think I am quite young. I ran away from home the day I was born."

Wendy asked him why.

"Because I heard my father saying that one day I would grow up to become a man. I don't ever want to grow up. I want always to be a little boy and have fun. So I ran away from home and went to live with the fairies in Kensington Gardens."

"Fairies!" cried Wendy. "Are there really fairies in Kensington Gardens?"

Chapter 4
Fairies

Peter's mention of fairies was just too exciting for Wendy. "How did fairies begin?" she asked.

Peter explained that fairies began when the first baby in the world laughed. "That laugh," he said, "broke into a thousand pieces and they all went skipping about until they became fairies. That was how they began."

"Is there a fairy for every boy and girl?" asked Wendy.

"There ought to be," said Peter. "But there isn't. The trouble is that lots of people don't believe in fairies. And each time someone says they don't believe in fairies, somewhere or other a fairy dies."

"How sad," said Wendy.

But Peter wasn't really bothered. He had lost interest in the conversation. Now, he was more interested in finding Tinker Bell. "You haven't seen Tink the fairy have you?"

"Peter!" she exclaimed. "You don't mean to

say there's a fairy in the room!"

"She was here," said Peter calmly. "Can you hear her?"

"The only sound I can hear," said Wendy, "is the tinkle of bells."

"That's the language of fairies," Peter explained. "They can speak properly, but usually they speak only in tinkles. Obviously, I can understand tinkles. I can understand every word she says."

"The sound is coming from the chest of drawers," said Wendy.

"Oh dear, how wonderful," laughed Peter. "I've shut her in the chest of drawers by mistake!"

Peter opened the drawer and freed Tinker Bell. She flew about the nursery, screaming in fury.

Wendy looked on in wonder. "I wish she was my fairy," she said.

"You're too ugly," tinkled Tink. "I am Peter's fairy and nobody else's."

What a good thing she was tinkling, rather than speaking normally. Wendy would have been so upset.

"Tink is a most impolite and jealous fairy," said Peter.

A most impolite and jealous fairy.

With that, Tinker Bell flew off angrily into the bathroom.

Wendy had lots more questions for Peter. "Where do you live now?" she asked.

"Sometimes I live in Kensington Gardens," he said, "but mostly I live with the Lost Boys, in Neverland."

"Who are they?" asked Wendy.

"The Lost Boys are the children who fell out of their baby carriages when their nurses weren't looking," he explained. "If no one claims them in seven days, they are sent off to Neverland. I'm their captain."

"Aren't there any girls in Neverland?" asked Wendy.

"Not many," said Peter. "Girls are much too clever to fall out of their baby carriages."

Wendy then asked Peter why he had come to her nursery.

"Oh that's quite simple," said Peter. "None of the Lost Boys know any stories."

"But why come to my house?" asked Wendy.

"The swallow birds, of course," replied Peter. "Surely you know why swallows build their nests in the eaves of your house?"

"No," replied Wendy.

"Because they want to hear the stories your mother tells you at night," he said. "And that's why I came. Your mother was telling a lovely story about someone called Cinderella the other night."

"How sad that the Lost Boys don't know any stories," said Wendy. "I'd love to tell them all the stories I know."

"Then you must," cried Peter excitedly. "I'll teach you to fly. You can come to Neverland."

"Oh, I could never fly," Wendy sighed.

"I could easily teach you," said Peter. "Then we could jump on the wind's back and go and talk to the stars."

"Oooh!" cried Wendy. She could hardly hide her excitement at the thought of it.

"We could fly to Neverland," said Peter. "You could see the mermaids too."

"Oh, how wonderful," laughed Wendy.

Now Peter started to talk very seriously. "You could come to Neverland and tuck us in bed at night and tell us stories. You could darn our socks and make pockets for our clothes. None of us have any pockets."

"Could I bring my brothers, John and Michael?" Wendy asked. "Could you teach them to fly, too?"

"I'll teach you to fly."

"I suppose I could," said Peter, reluctantly. "But I think we all need a mother in Neverland rather than your brothers."

But Wendy was already clambering over to wake her brothers. "Wake up! Wake up!" she shouted. "Peter Pan has come to teach us to fly."

Chapter 5
Come Away, Come Away!

John and Michael couldn't contain their excitement when they saw Peter.

"Can you really teach us to fly?" asked Michael.

"Of course I can," said Peter. "I can do anything."

"Tell me how," said Michael.

"Just stand on the edge of your bed and think nice thoughts," explained Peter. "Those thoughts should lift you into the air."

Then he showed them how he did it.

The three children tried it once, twice, and three times. They thought of ice cream, strawberries, and lollypops, but still they couldn't fly.

The mischievous Peter finally confessed that it needed more than just good thoughts to fly. "You'll need fairy dust as well," he said. "But I haven't any with me."

But that's where Peter was wrong. By chance, he had accidentally dipped his hand in fairy dust before he left Neverland that day. Now, as he moved around in the air, the dust sprinkled down on the children.

First little Michael started to float into the air, then John, and finally, Wendy.

"Look!" exclaimed Michael. "I'm flying!"

"Look at me!" cried John.

"And me!" laughed Wendy.

It was true. They were all flying—but not as well as Peter. They were just learners. At first, they kept kicking out too much and wobbling their heads. Peter tried to give Wendy special flying lessons, but jealous Tinker Bell returned from the bathroom and stopped him. It didn't worry Wendy. She was getting the hang of flying far quicker than the boys.

"Oh, I want to fly out into the sky," cried Michael.

"I want to fly to the moon," said John.

Wendy was a little concerned. What would her parents say if they flew away?

But Peter was very cunning. He wanted Wendy in Neverland so she could look after the Lost Boys and tell them stories.

"Think of the mermaids you'll see," he said. "Think of talking to the stars."

And just to convince the boys, he told them

31

They were all flying.

that there were pirates in Neverland, too. That was the final temptation.

"Pirates!" cried John, grabbing his Sunday hat from its hook. "Let's go at once!"

Just then, they heard Nana barking louder than ever. Nana knew something was up. She was now straining desperately at the rope that tied her. At last it broke.

In a moment, she had leapt the garden fence and was running down the road to No. 27. She crashed through the door, burst into the dining room, and flung up her paws, right in front of an astonished Mrs. Darling.

"Let's go at once!"

Mrs. Darling knew at once that something was badly wrong. Without a word she rushed into the street, followed by Mr. Darling and Nana. They looked up at the nursery window. It was open and the room was ablaze with light, but the most heart-gripping sight of all was four shadows circling round and round in the air, near the window.

Mr. and Mrs. Darling rushed inside and ran up the stairs.

They didn't hear the smallest star cry out, "Watch out, Peter! Grown-ups are coming!"

Peter knew there was not a moment to lose. "Come on!" he cried. "Follow me!"

He soared out into the cold night with Wendy, John, and Michael behind him. A moment later, Mr. and Mrs. Darling and Nana burst into the nursery.

The children and Peter had flown.

Chapter 6
Journey to Neverland

Second to the right and straight on till morning . . . Peter had said that was the way to Neverland. However, the last thing that Wendy, John, and Michael wanted was to fly in a straight line. Flying was too exciting for that.

They swooped down over villages and rivers. Then they were flying over a sea, diving down on ships and whales. They lost count of the number of seas and oceans they crossed, and how long they had been flying.

They did eat on the way. Peter chased birds that were carrying food that humans might like. Then he took it and shared it around.

They got tired at times. Young Michael kept falling asleep and tumbling to earth.

Time and time again, Peter swooped down to rescue him just before he hit the ground.

Then they would play 'follow my leader'. Peter took the lead and let the others chase him. Sometimes he dived down and scratched the backs of sharks swimming in the sea. John and Michael did it too, but Wendy was frightened the sharks would snap her up and swallow her.

At last Peter pointed with his finger to an island far below. "There it is," he said calmly. "That's Neverland!"

Wendy, John, and Michael looked down. Of course, they recognized it at once. They had seen it before, somewhere in their dreams.

"Look John! There's your lagoon and boat house!" shouted Wendy.

"Look Michael!" said John. "Isn't that your flamingo by the wigwam?"

"Yes!" he replied. "And I can see the Indians too."

"Look Wendy!" said John. "There's your house made of sewn leaves."

The sun was sinking. It was getting dark. Wendy and the boys were a little frightened now. Dark shadows grew longer. The sound of unfamiliar cries of wild animals echoed beneath them.

The three little Darlings flew closer to Peter. Now he was getting quite excited. Tinker Bell, who had traveled on his shoulder, awoke. She flew off to see what was happening on the island.

Swooping down over villages and rivers.

"Look down there," said John. "There's a pirate, asleep in the grass."

"There are bound to be more nearby, too," said Peter.

"Who's the pirate's captain?" asked Michael.

Peter's face became very stern and serious. "Hook," he said solemnly. "Captain James Hook. Never was there a more villainous pirate. He will be my sworn enemy until one of us is dead."

"What's he like?" John asked nervously.

"He's not as big as he was," said Peter.

"What do you mean?" asked Michael.

"I cut a bit off him during a sword fight once," laughed Peter.

"Which bit?" asked John.

"His right arm," was the reply.

"So he can't fight any more," said Wendy, who was getting a little tired of the boys having all the talk.

"Oh yes he can," said Peter. "He can fight with both hands. He has a sword in his left hand, and now he has a great iron hook instead of a right hand. And he claws people with it."

"Oooh!" cried Michael.

Just then Tinker Bell, her light shining

"There's a pirate, asleep in the grass."

brighter than ever, flew back to Peter and said she had seen the pirates dragging out their big cannon.

"They must have seen us," said Peter. "We'd better watch out."

"Wouldn't it be safer," said Wendy, "if Tinker Bell turned her light out so they couldn't see us?"

Peter replied that Tinker couldn't turn out her light. "It only goes out naturally when she falls asleep."

Then John came up with a good idea. Tinker could travel in the black top hat he had brought with him, so her light wouldn't be seen. She was quite happy to hide in that!

Suddenly, there was the loudest crash the three children had ever heard. Whoosh! A huge iron ball flew between Peter and Wendy.

The pirates had fired their cannon. Luckily, the ball missed everyone. But the force of the explosion sent Wendy flying high into the sky with Tinker Bell. Wendy didn't know where she was any more. Peter, John, and Michael were nowhere to be seen. She had to rely on Tinker Bell, who now took her chance.

Tink was so jealous of Wendy. She was worried in case she became Peter's best friend.

Poor Wendy didn't know that Tink hated her.

"Follow me and all will be well," called Tinker Bell, swooping away again.

Wendy did as she was told and followed the jealous fairy, little realizing that Tinker Bell was leading her to her doom. Then, without a word, Tink suddenly dived away from Wendy and vanished.

Wendy was alone and very frightened.

Chapter 7
Lost Boys, Pirates, and Indians

One of the strange things about Neverland was how quiet it was when Peter Pan was away from the island. None of the Lost Boys fought a single pirate when he was absent. The Indians didn't hunt the wild beasts and the fairies took an hour longer to get out of bed. But if you put an ear to the ground once Peter had returned, you would hear the island seething with life again.

That evening, as Peter Pan approached Neverland, the Lost Boys had heard a rumor that he might be on his way back. The number of Lost Boys on the island varied at any one time. It depended on how many had been killed in recent battles, or started to grow up and had to leave. There were six just then.

There was Tootles, who was not very brave. He usually turned up at battles when all was over and the blood had dried up. He was a kind boy and usually fell for other people's tricks; especially Tinker Bell's.

The Lost Boys.

Then there was Nibs, a happy young chap with a cocky nose rather like Peter's, and Slightly who made wooden whistles and danced a lot. Slightly always imagined he could remember the days before he became a Lost Boy. But, of course, he couldn't.

Curly, the fourth Lost Boy was a puzzle. If ever Peter wanted someone to blame for something, Curly always stood up and said he'd done it. He often stood up even when he hadn't done anything.

The other two Lost Boys were the Twins. We can't describe them in case we get the wrong one. Peter never quite understood what twins were. And because no one was allowed to know more than Peter, none of the other boys did either.

The Lost Boys lived in a wonderful secret home beneath the ground. How the pirates wanted to find out where that house was!

That evening the Lost Boys were very excited because of the rumors of Peter Pan's return. Everyone else on Neverland was excited, too. They were racing around the island, chasing each other. Because they were all going at the same speed, they never met.

The Lost Boys were in front, and the pirates

were on their trail. They could hear the pirates coming because they always sang the same dreadful pirate song.

> *"Avast below there, yo ho heave to,*
> *A-pirating we go,*
> *And if we're parted by a shot,*
> *We're sure to meet below."*

What a villainous crew! There was Cecco, who had escaped from prison to join Hook's men. Then there was Bill Jukes who was covered from head to toe with dreadful tattoos. Pete Cookson, said to be the brother of Black Hearted Murphy, came next. Behind him was Gentleman Starkey, who was very dainty in his ways of killing.

The other crew included the genial Irish Bosun Smee, who wore spectacles, and Noodler, whose hands were fixed on backwards.

In the midst of them came the blackest and most cruel-hearted pirate of them all, Captain James Hook. His hair was twisted into long black curls. His ice-cold blue eyes seemed so sad. But that was only because just then, he wasn't plunging his hook into anyone. If he had, he would have been smiling with blood-red

What a villainous crew!

eyes! The terrifying hook that had replaced his right arm made him look even more sinister.

Hook was only afraid of one thing ... crocodiles.

When Peter Pan had cut off Hook's arm in the fight, he had thrown it to a passing crocodile. The beast had eaten the arm and thoroughly enjoyed the taste of it. The crocodile now followed Hook everywhere. It wanted to taste the rest of him.

At least Captain Hook knew when the crocodile was close by. Soon after eating Hook's arm,

The crocodile followed Hook everywhere.

47

the crocodile had swallowed a clock. It was still ticking away in its stomach. The "tick-tock, tick-tock" gave Hook good warning of his presence.

Behind the pirates came the Indians from the Piccaninny tribe. They were on the warpath with tomahawks and knives. Great Big Little Panther was their chief and Tiger Lily his proud princess. Lean Wolf and Big Bear were their bravest fighters.

Behind them came the wild beasts looking for a meal. There were lions, tigers, and all sorts of bloodthirsty creatures.

And right behind them came a single crocodile.

Tick-tock! Tick-tock! Tick-tock!

Chapter 8
Shoot the Wendy Bird

It was very exhausting, with everyone following everyone else. The Lost Boys stopped first and retired to their home under the ground.

Each boy had his own secret entrance. There were seven hollow trees above the house; one each for Peter and the six Lost Boys. To get into the home under the ground, each boy simply climbed into his tree and then slid down it.

The reason that there were seven trees was because every boy was a different size. The boys had to have a tree which fitted them, or else they might get stuck on the way down.

As soon as the pirates realized that the Lost Boys had vanished, they stopped following them. Captain Hook sat down to rest on a large mushroom. "I wonder when Peter Pan will return," he said. "I shall have his blood when he does."

Suddenly, Hook leapt from the mushroom. "I'm on fire!" he shouted.

Indeed he was. Without knowing it, he had sat on a very special mushroom. It was put there to disguise the chimney of the Lost Boys' home, under the ground. Smoke was now billowing from his trousers. He jumped into the nearest stream to put himself out. Steam and smoke hissed around him.

Hook was most curious about the mushroom. It didn't take him long to find out that it hid a chimney. He heard voices coming from it and leaned down to listen. He could hear Tootles talking.

"I'm pretty sure Peter will be back with us by tonight," he was saying.

Captain Hook was delighted. Not only was his greatest enemy coming back to Neverland, but he had also stumbled on the Lost Boys' secret house . . . not that he had found a way in yet. But his joy didn't last long. Another sound filled his ears.

Tick-tock! Tick-tock! Tick-tock!

It was the crocodile.

"Everyone back to the ship!" screamed Hook, running for his life.

When the boys came out there was no sign of anyone, except Tinker Bell, who had just flown down.

"I'm on fire!"

"Where's Peter?" the Lost Boys asked as one.

Jealous Tinker Bell then told a terrible lie.

"Peter is on his way," she said, "but he sent me ahead with some special orders. There is a dangerous creature called a Wendy Bird that has just reached Neverland. Peter wants her shot down immediately."

Tootles, who was always keen to please Peter, raced away to get his bow and arrow. Then he set off in pursuit of the Wendy Bird.

In the meantime, poor Wendy was still very lost. There was no sign of Peter, or John and Michael. She had flown this way and that until she was almost exhausted.

She didn't see Tootles below her with his bow and arrow. She didn't see him shoot it, either. But she did feel a sting in her chest as the arrow hit and she began to tumble to earth.

A few minutes later, poor foolish Tootles was standing like a conqueror over Wendy's body. The arrow was still sticking out of her chest. All the other Lost Boys gathered around her.

"I have shot the Wendy Bird," said Tootles, proudly. "Peter will be so pleased with me."

"This is no bird," said Nibs, looking down at Wendy.

Poor Wendy was still very lost.

"It's a lady," said Tootles.

It was at that tragic moment that the boys heard a familiar sound. It was Peter crowing; he always signaled his return that way. The boys were still crowded around Wendy, hiding her completely when he landed.

"Hello boys," cried Peter as he arrived with John and Michael. "I'm back and I have great news. I have at last brought a mother for you all. She has lots of stories to tell us at night."

There was silence. Tootles face turned white with horror.

Curly spoke first. "Was it the Wendy Bird that was to be our mother?" he asked.

"She is not a bird," said Peter. "But Wendy is her name."

Poor Tootles burst into tears. "I have killed our mother," he sobbed.

The Lost Boys moved back to reveal Wendy's body.

Tootles took the arrow from Wendy's chest. He gave it to Peter and he dropped to his knees, and bared his own chest. "Strike, Peter," said Tootles. "Take my life in return."

Just then everyone heard a voice say, "Poor Tootles."

Chapter 9
The Wendy House

It was Wendy's voice. She was alive, but badly stunned by her fall to earth.

"She lives!" cried Tootles.

Peter rushed across to her. He saw immediately what had happened. "The arrow hit my kiss," he said. "I gave her a kiss and it saved her life."

What Peter was talking about was the button that he had given Wendy when they first met. She had hung it from a chain around her neck and the arrow had hit the button.

There was a sudden wailing sound from above them.

"Listen to Tink," said Curly. "She is sad because Wendy is still alive."

Peter then heard the story of how jealous Tink had wanted Wendy killed.

He was furious. "Tinker Bell," he shouted. "You're not my friend any more. Now be gone from me forever."

Tinker Bell flew down to his shoulder and begged to be allowed to stay. Only when Wendy pleaded on her behalf did Peter change his mind. "Alright," he said, "you needn't be gone forever; just a whole week."

"If I must," said Tink sadly.

Peter and the boys decided that it might hurt Wendy if they moved her. So they decided to build a cottage around her.

"What sort of house would you like?" Peter asked.

Wendy started to sing:

"I wish I had a pretty house,
The littlest ever seen,
With funny little red walls,
And roof of mossy green."

So that's what they built. And when it was finished, Peter sang a verse:

"We've built the little walls and roof,
And made a lovely door,
So tell us, Mother Wendy,
What are you wanting more?"

Wendy started singing again:

"The arrow hit my kiss."

"Oh really, next I think I'll have,
Little windows all about,
With roses peeping in, you know,
And babies peeping out."

They found roses to cover the cottage, but the only babies to be seen were really just the Lost Boys. So Peter sang another verse:

"We've made the roses peeping out,
The babies are at the door,
We cannot make ourselves you know,
'Cos we've been made before."

All that was needed now was a chimney. Peter had an idea. He snatched the top hat from John's head, knocked out the top and put that on the roof.

Peter decided to knock on the door and see if anyone was inside. So he did. The next moment the door opened, and there was Wendy. She was a little better already.

"This is the most darling cottage," she said. "I want to live here forever."

"And we want you to stay forever and be our mother," said the Lost Boys as one.

The Wendy House

"This is the most darling cottage."

59

"Right!" said Wendy. "You had better all come in if you can, and I'll tell you the story of Cinderella."

So they all squeezed in to hear her story.

Afterwards, the Lost Boys returned to the house under the ground, to sleep.

But Peter stayed behind to guard Wendy in her house. He stood outside all night with his little sword drawn.

When Wendy was fully recovered, the Lost Boys moved her to the house under the ground. How she missed the little Wendy House. But sometimes she went to stay in it at weekends.

Wendy came to love her new home under the ground. It was really just one big room. There was a table with mushrooms for chairs all around it, and an enormous fireplace in the center of the room. A washing line was stretched beside it. This was where Wendy hung the washing to dry.

There was one great bed where all the Lost Boys, and John and Michael slept. By day it leaned against the wall. They let it down when it was bedtime.

Tinker Bell had her own tiny little room. It could be shut off from the main room by a curtain. Her room was covered in mirrors. Tink was a very vain fairy.

Wendy busied herself for most of the day with cooking. The Lost Boys' favorite foods included bread-fruit, yams, coconuts, baked pig, mammee-apples, pappa-rolls, and bananas. They washed all that down with great jugs of lime juice.

Wendy would sew and darn the children's clothing after they had gone to bed.

And remember the pet wolf that she used to dream about when she was at home? The Indians had a pet wolf and when it heard that Wendy had arrived on Neverland, it went to see her.

Wendy loved that wolf. It came to visit her most days, but it always stayed at the Indian camp at night.

Chapter 10
The Mermaids' Lagoon

Wendy had lost all sense of time after arriving in Neverland. She never worried about what her mother and father might be thinking. She knew the nursery window would always be open so that she and her brothers could return.

There were new adventures every day for the three of them. There was the day that the Indians attacked the Lost Boys at Peter Pan Gulch, and the night that the Indians made an attack on the house under the ground. Two of the Indians were so fat they got stuck in the tree trunks!

Then there were the poisonous cakes the pirates made. They placed them all over Neverland, hoping Peter would eat one of them. But Wendy always found them first and hid them.

And one windy day, the nest of the Never Bird fell out of a tree and into the Mermaids' Lagoon. The nest floated off with the mother bird still sitting on the eggs, but it didn't seem to worry the bird at all. The father bird flew out regularly with food and each day, one of the Lost Boys would swim out to check that the mother and her eggs were alright. The Never Bird was very grateful to them.

There is another story about the Mermaids' Lagoon. And this one I must tell you in full.

The children often spent long summer days on the lagoon, swimming or just floating about. Beautiful mermaids with long silver tails lived there. They weren't very friendly though.

Wendy never had a civil word from the mermaids during her time on the island.

But she did love to watch them when they sat on Marooners' Rock. They used to bask in the sun, combing their hair. When it got too hot, they would slip into the lagoon.

Sometimes the mermaids swam off to look around the lagoon. Then Peter, Wendy, John and Michael, and the Lost Boys would swim out and sit on Marooners' Rock themselves.

One evening they were all on the rock, when Wendy suddenly saw a small boat coming toward them. It was a pirate boat being rowed by Bosun Smee and Gentleman Starkey.

It was just starting to get dark and mist was

Swimming out to check on the mother.

rising off the lagoon. Smee and Starkey had lit their lamps and in the murky half-light, Peter saw that there was someone else in the boat with them. It was the Indian princess, Tiger Lily. She was bound hand and foot. She had been captured by the pirates.

Wendy, Peter, and the boys all slipped off the rock and swam across to a bank of weed. They hid there and waited to see what the pirates were up to.

"Here's Marooners' Rock," said Smee. "Now all we've got to do is to throw Tiger Lily ashore and leave her to die. Maroon her! That's what the captain ordered."

It was a pirate boat.

Just then, Peter had an idea. He could cleverly imitate most people's voices. "Ahoy there!" he shouted, in Captain Hook's voice. It was a perfect imitation.

"It's the captain!" said Smee. "Sounds like he's quite close to us."

"We're just putting the girl ashore, Captain," called out Starkey.

"Set her free!" was the reply.

"Free her, Captain?" asked a very puzzled Smee.

"Yes," said the voice from the ever-darkening shadows of the lagoon. "Cut her bonds and let her go."

"But, Captain . . ."

"Do it this moment, Smee," replied the Captain's voice, "or I'll plunge me hook into you."

Smee quickly untied the ropes and Tiger Lily slipped into the water and swam away.

Then another voice rang out. "Ahoy there!" This time it was the real Captain Hook on another small boat. As his boat came closer, Wendy got her first look at the villainous pirate. It was almost dark now, but in the light of his lantern, Wendy saw his hook grip the side of the boat. His evil, swarthy face looked terrifying.

"There's trouble ahead," snarled Hook.

"Set her free!"

"The Lost Boys have found a mother. They call her Wendy."

"Oh, evil day!" wailed Starkey.

"What's a mother?" asked Smee.

Wendy felt quite sorry for Smee. If she could have a pirate for a pet, then Smee would be the one.

"That's a mother," said Starkey, pointing to the Never Bird, floating by on its nest.

"I'd like a mother," said Smee.

"Pirates don't need mothers," said Captain Hook, although deep down he wished he had a mother just as much as Smee. "I'll tell you what, if we can seize Pan and the children, we could make them all walk the plank. Then we'd keep Wendy to be our mother."

Wendy heard every word. She could hardly control herself. The thought of being mother to the terrifying pirates made her shiver.

It was then that Hook asked where Tiger Lily was. At first, both Smee and Starkey thought he was joking.

"Where is she?" said Smee. "What do you mean? We let her go."

"You let her go!" screamed Hook.

He was as furious as Starkey and Smee had ever seen him.

Chapter 11
The Battle of Marooners' Rock

Starkey and Smee did their best to explain why they had let Tiger Lily go.

"We let her go on your orders," said Starkey. "You called to us from across the water."

"Brimstone and gall!" roared Hook. "I never gave such an order!"

"This is all very strange," said Starkey.

"Strange indeed," said Hook with a shiver. "There are spirits haunting the lagoon tonight."

That was too much for Peter. He'd been bursting to crow. So now he called out in Hook's voice again. "Odds, bobs, hammers, and tongues," he called. "Fee, fi, fo, fum . . ."

Smee and Starkey clung to each other in terror.

"Who are you, stranger?" called out Hook.

"'Tis, I, Captain Hook," answered Peter.

"You're not!" cried Hook. "You're a lying rogue."

"Brimstone and gall," replied Peter, using Hook's own words. "Say that again and I'll throw my anchor at you!"

"If you are Hook," said the Captain, "then come and tell me who I am."

"You're a codfish," was the reply. "You're a smelly codfish."

Smee and Starkey were shaking with fear now. "Have we been captained by a codfish all this time?" asked Smee.

Peter finally couldn't contain himself any more. He burst out laughing.

Hook recognized who his tormentor was immediately.

"It's Pan!" he screamed at Smee and Starkey. "Get him—dead or alive!"

Peter was all too ready for a battle. And Marooners' Rock was where he was going to fight it. "Leave this to me," he shouted to Wendy and the boys. "I can handle Hook, Smee, and Starkey all by myself."

"Oh, do be careful," said Wendy.

"Wendy, take the boys and swim to the shore," said Peter. "The tide is coming in and it will soon be too strong for the boys to swim against."

With that, he swam off towards Marooners' Rock.

"Who are you, stranger?"

When Peter reached the rock, Smee and Starkey were already there. He knocked down Starkey with a single blow of his fist. That was enough for Starkey. He dived off the rock and swam to safety.

Smee was not the best pirate fighter, mainly because he could not see very well, even with his glasses on. He quickly fell off the rock and was last seen swimming off toward Starkey's boat.

Now, where was Hook?

At that moment Hook had reached the rock and was sliding up toward Peter, like a snake. Peter turned and saw him. With Hook crawling along his belly, Peter could have cut him in two with the sword he carried quite easily. Yet even at that moment, Peter wanted a fair fight. He reached down and offered a hand to help him up.

Hook was no gentlemen. He bit Peter's hand and then caught him three terrible blows with his hook. Peter fell to the ground, helpless.

Hook would have run Peter through with his sword there and then, but suddenly, he heard something.

Tick-tock! Tick-tock! Tick-tock!

It was the crocodile.

Hook shivered like a jelly, dived into the water, and swam desperately toward his boat.

Peter fell to the ground, helpless.

He only just made it, as the crocodile narrowly missed taking a patch out of his trousers. He rowed away as fast as he could.

By the time the battle was over, the incoming tide was almost lapping at the top of Marooners' Rock, with Peter injured, alone, and unable to swim to shore. Without help, he would soon drown. Looking out from the shore, there was nothing that Wendy and the boys could do.

Yet, was Peter scared? Not a bit of it.

"To drown in Mermaids' Lagoon will be an awfully big adventure!" he cried boldly.

Peter heard the sounds of the mermaids returning to their bedrooms in the Coral Caves under the lagoon. It was no use calling out to them for help.

He dimly became aware of something still moving out on the lagoon. He thought it was a piece of paper. Slowly, it came a little closer. Now he saw what it was; the Never Bird floating on its nest!

Peter Pan and the boys had helped keep her safe when her nest had fallen into the water. Now the bird had come to try and save Peter.

Chapter 12
The Never Bird to the Rescue

The poor Never Bird had exhausted herself by paddling against the tide. She called out to Peter and told him what she wanted him to do. And Peter called out to her to ask what she was saying. But, of course, they did not understand each other's language.

"I want you to get into my nest," said the Never Bird, in Never Bird talk. "And then you can drift ashore. But I am too exhausted to get any closer to you. You'll have to swim."

"What are you quacking about?" asked Peter.

Peter and the bird became rather angry at each other.

"You dunderhead!" screeched the bird. "Why don't you do as you're told?"

"What a strange language," said Peter.

Suddenly, the bird flew off her nest, deserting the eggs. Then, flying around above Peter, she pointed at the nest with her beak, and then pointed at Peter. At last he understood what she was trying to say.

Peter knew that the bird was prepared to sacrifice her eggs for him. She wanted him to use her nest to sail to shore. It wasn't large enough to carry Peter, the bird and the eggs. But it was large enough to carry Peter by himself.

Peter didn't want to see the bird lose her eggs, so he looked around to see if there was anything he could do to save them. He saw that Starkey had accidentally left his pirate hat behind on the rock. This gave him an idea.

Wounded as he was, Peter managed to swim out to the nest and pull it to the rock.

Then he carefully removed the eggs and placed them inside Starkey's hat. Next, he floated the hat onto the water, bowed to the bird and indicated that she should now resume sitting on the eggs.

The Never Bird screamed out her admiration for Peter, and in turn, he crowed with pride. The bird clambered aboard and was soon sitting happily on her eggs again.

Peter waved goodbye and then boarded the bird's nest. He picked out one of the nest's bigger sticks and hung his shirt on it, for a sail.

They did not understand each other's language.

He was soon being blown toward the shore. The Never Bird waved and then vanished into the night, sitting comfortably on her eggs inside Starkey's upturned hat.

Wendy, John and Michael, and the Lost Boys were delighted that Peter was safe.

In the days ahead, Gentleman Starkey often came to the shore of the lagoon. He would have liked his hat back, but the Never Bird refused. It was far too comfortable.

To this day, children always notice how Never Birds build their nests to the same design as Starkey's hat. They have a deep nest

He was blown toward the shore.

and a rim around the edge for the young to run around.

One important result of the battle on the lagoon was that the Indians made peace with Peter Pan and the Lost Boys. Peter had, after all, saved Tiger Lily's life.

Now, there was nothing the Indians wouldn't do for Peter Pan and his friends. They even took to guarding the house under the ground each night from attacks by the pirates.

The Indians were on guard on what became known as the Night of Nights.

That evening, Peter had left the house to find out the time. If you wanted to know the time in Neverland, you went and found the ticking crocodile. Then you stayed with him until the clock struck the hour.

Wendy and all the other children were having their evening meal. Well, actually they were having a make-believe tea, and what with their chatter and laughing, the noise was deafening.

"Silence!" cried Wendy for the twentieth time.

The noise just got louder.

"Have you finished your milk, Slightly?" asked Wendy.

"Not quite empty, Mummy," Slightly said, looking into his imaginary mug.

"He hasn't even begun to drink his milk," sneaked Nibs.

That was telling on someone, and wasn't allowed. It gave the other person the right to make an official complaint.

"I complain of Nibs," yelled Slightly.

He didn't get a chance to complain because John stood up and asked if he could sit in Father's chair, which of course was the chair that Peter Pan sat in.

"He's not your father," said Slightly. "Fathers have to grow up and Peter says he will never do that."

Tootles put up his hand and asked if he could play Father. He was the gentlest of the Lost Boys and Wendy said very quietly that he couldn't. But once Tootles had started saying something, he tended to carry on.

"As I can't be Father," he said, "will Michael let me be the baby?"

"No I won't," said Michael. "I'm the baby."

Tootles still carried on. "If I can't be baby can I be one of the twins?"

"No," said the Twins together. "We're twins and if there were three of us, we wouldn't be twins."

80

They were having a make-believe tea.

At last Tootles was silent. But now the shouting and screaming continued with everyone else talking over each other.

"Oh dear. Oh dear," said Wendy. "I sometimes think that children are more trouble than they are worth!"

Chapter 13
Wendy's Story

Soon after, Peter returned with the time for Wendy and some nuts for the boys.

"Peter, you do spoil the boys so," said Wendy. "Just like a father!"

Peter had made it quite clear that he didn't want to be father. Yet he did like the idea of bringing everyone treats. It made him feel very generous indeed.

Later that night, when Peter and all the boys were in bed, Wendy told them a special story.

"There once was a lady and a gentleman," she began. "They were called Mr. and Mrs. Darling and they lived at No. 14. They had three children who were looked after by a nurse called Nana, who was a dog."

Nibs interrupted to say that he thought it an excellent story so far. Peter wasn't enjoying the story at all. He had a bad memory and he couldn't remember whether he had heard the story or whether it was a story about him. He could vaguely remember a dog called Nana biting off his shadow.

"Now one night," said Wendy, "Nana misbehaved and Mr. Darling tied her up in the yard. So all the children flew out of the nursery window and went to Neverland, where the Lost Boys lived."

"I thought that is where they would fly to," said Curly.

Wendy continued. "Now children, I want you to consider the feelings of the unhappy parents those children left behind. Think of those three empty beds in the house."

"It's awfully sad," said one of the Twins.

"I don't see how this story can have a happy ending," said the other.

"You shouldn't worry about that," said Wendy, lovingly. "A mother's love is so great. This story will surely have a happy ending."

"You're my mother," said Tootles, "and I know you love me no end."

"And me," said Nibs.

"And me," said everyone else except Peter. He hated it when people got soppy and talked of love.

Wendy continued. "The children in my story knew that Mrs. Darling loved them all. They

Wendy told them a special story.

knew that she would leave the nursery window open for them if they wanted to come back."

Nibs wanted to know if the three children ever did go back.

"Only the future can tell that," said Wendy. "But I think they will. They will stay away for some time and have lots of fun and adventures. Then they will go home because their mother and father love them so much."

Peter suddenly interrupted. "You are wrong about mothers," he said. "Long ago I thought my mother would always keep the nursery window open for me. And I stayed away for moons and moons and moons. And when I did go back, the window was closed and barred. My mother had forgotten all about me and there was another boy sleeping in my bed."

Michael began to cry. "Please, Wendy, let's go home. Mother and Father may have forgotten us already."

"Yes," said John. "We must go home."

"I think you are right," said Wendy at last. "It is time for us to go home."

"Not tonight," said Nibs. "You must make us breakfast in the morning before you go."

The Lost Boys were heartbroken. They couldn't bear the thought of losing Wendy.

"Please, Wendy, let's go home."

Peter was terribly upset but he didn't show
it at all. "If you want to go home, then you
must," he said, as coolly as if she had asked him
to pass the nuts.

He certainly wasn't going to show Wendy
how much he cared. He was in a very bad
temper, so he climbed up his tree and went
outside to be on his own for a while. When he
came back in, he found Nibs had taken Wendy
prisoner.

"She can't leave us!" said Nibs, picking up
some rope to tie her with.

"No, she can't," said Slightly. "We shall keep
her tied up like Nana in the story."

Chapter 14
Pirates and Indians

Brave Tootles stepped forward to protect Wendy from Nibs.

"I am an English gentleman," he said, "and I will not have Wendy treated like this. Let her go this moment!"

Peter pretended that he didn't care what happened to Wendy. "I'm sure the Indians will escort you through the forest," he said, "and then I will get Tinker Bell to fly with you across the sea. Nibs, get Tinker Bell this minute."

Nibs went to Tink's hideaway behind the curtain. He had to knock twice before he got an answer. In fairy talk, she told him that she had been sleeping and didn't want to be disturbed.

In truth, Tinker Bell had been listening to every word from behind the curtain. She was delighted that Wendy was going home, but she didn't want the job of escorting her across the sea.

"Let her go this moment!"

Nibs told her to get up. Tink refused.

"Right," said Nibs. "If you don't get up, I shall open the curtains so everyone can see you in your nightdress."

Tinker Bell was out of bed and dressed in a minute. "Who said I wasn't getting up?" she cried.

Wendy had become very tearful now. She had come to love the Lost Boys like a real mother.

"Dear ones," she said. "Why don't you all come with John and Michael and me? I'm sure my parents would adopt you."

Tinker Bell didn't want to be disturbed.

91

The boys jumped for joy at that idea. "Peter, can we go?" they all asked as one.

"You may go," said Peter, grimly. "But, of course, I will stay here."

"Please," begged Wendy, "you must come with the others."

"No!" he said very firmly.

And as if to show that losing Wendy meant nothing to him, he danced around the floor.

"We might find your mother," said Wendy.

"No," sulked Peter. "She will make me old. Now everyone must leave. No fuss. No kissing. No blubbering!"

Then Peter, politely but coldly, held out his hand for Wendy to shake. "Goodbye, Wendy," he said, as if he was talking to a piece of wood.

Wendy burst into tears, but even that didn't stop Peter from being so cruel.

"Come on everyone," he said. "It's time to leave."

Peter may not have been crying on the outside. But if you could have found a way into his little head, you would have seen that it was flooded with tears.

"Are you ready, Tink?" asked Peter. "Don't forget to come straight back after you've seen the girl and her brothers across the sea."

Tink couldn't wait to escort Wendy, John, and Michael across the sea. She darted into Slightly's tree and flew out of the home under the ground.

The next thing everyone heard was a loud shriek coming from Tinker Bell. She had reached the top just as the dastardly Captain Hook made an attack on the Indians guarding the home. Up above the ground, the air was filled with shrieks and the sound of steel on steel.

Below, there was dead silence. Mouths opened wide in surprise. Wendy fell on her knees, her arms extending toward Peter as though asking him to help them all. Peter wasn't quite sure what to do. One part of him wanted to go up and fight, but he decided to wait and see what happened before he joined the battle.

The pirate attack on the Indians had come as a great surprise. It was already late in the evening and everyone in Neverland had signed an agreement promising not to fight anyone after teatime. Captain Hook had broken all the rules of the game—and he took a fearful revenge on the Indians for siding with Peter Pan.

Captain Hook made an attack on the Indians.

Tinker Bell was now sitting in a tree looking down on the scene. And what a horrible scene it was. Gathered around the brave Tiger Lily were a dozen of her stoutest warriors. They saw the pirates coming in huge numbers. The Indians knew that they would have a terrible fight on their hands that night.

Hook and his men easily won the battle, but the Indians did have some success. Lean Wolf chased a pirate called Alf Mason all the way into the lagoon. Then terrifying Tim Turley had his sword broken in two by the tomahawk of Great Big Little Panther.

It was Great Big Little Panther who finally cut his way through the pirates so that Tiger Lily and a few other Indians could escape to fight another day.

One might have imagined that Captain Hook would have been delighted with his success. But no! The night's work was not over. It was not the Indians he had come to destroy. They were just bees to be smoked out of the hive so Hook could get at the honey.

It was Peter Pan that Captain Hook wanted . . .

Chapter 15
Captured!

Peter was such a small boy that it might be a puzzle to some why Hook hated him so much. True, he had cut off Hook's arm and thrown it to the crocodile. But even that couldn't really explain his dislike for Peter.

The truth is that there was something about Peter that drove the pirate into a frenzy. It was not Peter's courage. It was not his good looks. There is no beating about the bush on this matter. For we all know well what it really was.

It was Peter's cockiness and his constant crowing.

They got on Captain Hook's nerves. They made his iron claw twitch. And at night Peter's cockiness and crowing irritated the pirate like an insect which had got into his bedclothes. While Peter still lived, Hook was a tortured man.

Now that the Indians had scattered, the question for Hook was how to get down into the house under the ground . . . or how to persuade the children to come out.

Down below, everyone had been listening to the noisy battle going on above their heads. Now all was silent again. Peter wondered which side had won. "If the Indians have won," he said, "then they will beat out their victory on their tom-tom drums."

Unfortunately for Peter, Hook had been listening at one of the trees. He sent Smee to find a tom-tom. He returned a moment later with the drum. A dreadful smile crossed Hook's face as he ordered Smee to beat out a victory roll on the drum.

Peter heard the drum and shouted out in delight. "The Indians have won," he cried. "Can't you hear the tom-toms?"

The doomed children answered with a cheer that was music to the ears of the black-hearted villain above.

"Come on then," called Peter. "It's safe for all of you to leave now. I'm going to bed."

"Are you sure you won't come with us, Peter?" asked Wendy, one last time.

Peter simply shook his head and headed off to bed.

Everyone except Peter went to their trees,

Listening at one of the trees.

and climbed up toward the battlefield above.

The first to emerge was Curly. Oh, disaster of disasters! He clambered straight into the arms of the pirate Cecco, who flung him to Smee, who flung him to Starkey, who flung him to Bill Jukes, who flung him to Noodler. Poor Curly was flung from one pirate to the next until he finally landed at the feet of Hook.

Hook had a pirate at every tree and all the boys were plucked from their trees in the same ruthless manner. Wendy was treated differently. With remarkable politeness, Hook raised his hat and offered to escort her to where all the others were now being tied up and gagged.

Each boy was tied in such a way that it would be impossible to fly away. They were all roped, doubled up with their chins on their knees, and carried off to Hook's pirate ship.

Wendy was escorted to the ship by Cecco.

Only Hook stayed behind. And now he headed for Slightly's tree. It was the largest tree and Hook had already measured himself. He might just fit inside it.

First, he listened. All was silent. Now he started to worry. Was Peter asleep? Or was he waiting for him with dagger in hand? There

The first to emerge was Curly.

was only one way to find out. He had to go down.

Hook let slip his cloak to the ground. Then, biting his lip, he stepped into the tree.

He was a brave man, but for one moment he had to stop to wipe his sweating brow. Then silently, he slipped down the tree.

There was no dagger waiting for him at the bottom. It was quite dim and it took him some while to become accustomed to the light. Then at last he saw what he had sought for so long. On the great bed, Peter lay fast asleep.

Chapter 16
The Poisoned Medicine

Peter was completely unaware of what had happened to everyone above ground.

After Wendy and the boys had left, he had gone to bed and played a tune on his pipes. He completely ignored some medicine that Wendy had poured into a glass for him before leaving.

"Huh!" he said, sulkily. "I don't need any of Wendy's medicine."

The truth was that he would have loved Wendy to stay and tuck him up in bed at night. That evening he made sure no one could see or hear him and then burst into tears. He cried himself to sleep.

He was so tired he didn't even dream. One of his arms had dropped over the edge of the bed, and one leg was arched up. The unfinished part of a silent crow lay stranded on his mouth, which was open and showing his pearly little teeth.

He cried himself to sleep.

That was how Captain Hook found him. The pirate stood silently at the foot of the bed, looking at his enemy. Now, did Captain Hook feel sorry for the boy? Did he feel it was unfair to kill a sleeping boy?

Captain Hook, as we know, was not wholly evil. It's said he loved flowers and sweet music. He could be kind to little girls. He was, perhaps, two men. If his better self had been in control, he might have left Peter where he was and waited until he awoke.

Sadly, it was the other side that ruled him that night. Hook could only see the most annoying and cockiest boy who ever lived. That steeled his heart. He saw the medicine glass beside Peter's bed. He crept slowly across the room. Once beside the sleeping boy, he took out a small bottle from his coat pocket.

The bottle contained a mixture of all the most dreadful poisons he had collected on his travels. It was probably the most deadly poison in Neverland. He added five drops of it to Peter's glass.

With one final gloating look at the boy, Hook went back to the tree and wormed his way to the surface again. He emerged from the top with a dreadful look of triumph on his face.

Then he put on his hat, wound his cloak around him, and disappeared into the night.

Peter slept on. It was ten o'clock by the crocodile when he awoke the next morning. Tinker Bell was sitting on the end of his bed. She had returned to the house just a few moments earlier.

Half asleep, Peter picked up the glass of medicine and raised it to his lips. For Tink, there was no time for words, for she had heard Hook muttering about what he had done as he ran through the forest. With one lightning

He added five drops to Peter's glass.

105

movement, she flew onto the side of the glass
and drained the whole of its contents.

"How dare you drink my medicine!" Peter
shouted angrily.

But Tink did not answer. She was already
dying.

"What's the matter?" asked Peter, suddenly
afraid.

"Wendy and the boys have been captured
and Hook poisoned your medicine," said Tink
weakly. "And now I'm going to be dead."

"Oh Tink," said Peter softly. "Did you drink
it to save me?"

"Yes, Peter, I did," replied Tink wearily.

"But why?" asked Peter.

Tinker Bell's wings could hardly carry her
now, but she flitted down onto his shoulder and
gave his chin a loving bite.

"You silly boy!" she said, tottering off to her
own bedroom and lying down on the bed.

Tink's light was becoming dimmer each
moment. She could hardly speak, but she was
trying to say something.

At last, Peter understood.

She was saying that she might get well again
if children truly believed in fairies.

Peter flung out his arms. There were no

The Poisoned Medicine

She was trying to say something.

children in the house under the ground, but he cried out to all children in the world who might be in their beds, dreaming of Neverland.

"Do you believe in fairies?" he shouted.

Tink sat up in her bed, listening to what her fate might be.

Peter shouted again. "If you believe in fairies, clap your hands. Don't let Tinker Bell die!"

Many did clap.

Some didn't. They knew what a jealous little fairy Tink could be.

However, enough children had clapped and Tink was saved. First her voice grew strong again and then she popped out of bed. Then she was flashing through every room, as cheerful as ever.

She never thought of thanking the ones who had clapped and saved her. But she would have liked to have got hold of the ones who hadn't.

"And now to rescue Wendy," said Peter.

The moon was riding high across the sky when Peter, sword in hand, emerged from the home under the ground. A deathly silence covered the island. The crocodile passed him, crawling quietly ever closer to its prey.

"It's Hook or me this time!" Peter cried out angrily.

Now, he slithered forward like a snake in the grass. Then he darted through a shaft of moonlight. One finger was on his lip and his dagger was at the ready.

Peter was frightfully happy.

Chapter 17
The Jolly Roger

Hook's pirate ship, the *Jolly Roger*, was moored in Kidd's Creek, beside the sea. The ship was wrapped in a blanket of mist. There was no sound except the whirring of the sewing machine that Smee was using to mend a jacket.

A few of the pirates were silently leaning over the side of the ship. The battle earlier that evening had exhausted them.

Suddenly, Hook appeared on deck. This was his hour of triumph. For sure, Peter Pan had been poisoned by now. And all the other Lost Boys were on the ship and about to walk the plank. Yet, despite his success, he was still not a happy man. He was deeply sad. It was because he was so terribly alone.

This strange creature of the sea was never more alone than when his crew of pirates were around him. They were just riff-raff; flotsam and jetsam and rubbish of the sea. He did not really like them at all.

Aboard the Jolly Roger

They knew him as Captain Hook, yet that wasn't his real name. To reveal who he truly was would shock them all. As a boy, he had gone to a famous school for the sons of the rich. He had learned all the school traditions; how to swagger as you walked, how to talk down to lesser folk.

This man was clever enough to have become a president. So what had he done that sent him tumbling into a life as a pirate who haunted the seven seas?

Nobody knew for sure. Some said it was because he had fallen in love with a young actress and had his heart broken. That had made him run away to sea. Others thought he might have gambled away the family fortune, and taken to pirating to recover his wealth.

Whatever it was, he had turned his back on his own kind and become the most famous pirate of his day.

Hook's past was like a claw within him; a claw far sharper than his iron hook. The claw gnawed away at him, always reminding him that he might have lived a better life. So never envy Captain Hook. His life was an unhappy one. Hook was doomed never to be loved.

Now, even in his moment of glory, there was

no pleasure in his life. When no one was listening, he whispered to himself, "Why don't children ever love me?"

Hook looked at Smee. He tried to puzzle out why people liked Smee. There was not a child on board the *Jolly Roger* who did not already love the man, and that included Wendy and all the Lost Boys, now held prisoner on the ship. Why, Michael had even tried on Smee's spectacles.

Hook could be a cruel man, but even he was not so cruel as to tell Smee how much he was liked. That would have been very unkind. Smee liked to be seen as the toughest pirate of them all.

Just then, the pirates broke into a noisy song.

"Silence, you scoundrels," roared Hook, "or you can join the boys on the plank."

There was a sudden silence again.

"Now," said Hook, "are all the children chained up so they can't fly away?"

"Aye! Aye!" they answered as one.

"Right," snarled Hook. "Then bring them up on deck."

The wretched prisoners, all except Wendy, were dragged from the hold of the ship and lined up in front of Hook.

Why did people like Smee?

"Now then my bullies," he said at last. "Four of you will walk the plank tonight, but I have room for two cabin boys. Which of you will it be? Which two of you want to become pirates?"

Chapter 18
Tick-tock! Tick-tock! Tick-tock!

Captain Hook glared at young Tootles. "Well, my boy," he asked. "Would you rather become my cabin boy or walk the plank?"

"I don't know what to say, Sir," said Tootles quietly. "If I had a mother, I don't think she would let me become a pirate."

Tootles turned to Slightly and asked if his mother would want him to be a pirate. "I don't think so," said Slightly. "What about you, Twins?"

"I don't think so," said the first twin.

"Nor me," said the second.

Captain Hook lost his temper at all the chitchat. "Stow this gabble," he roared, grabbing hold of John at the same time. "What about you, boy? Didn't you ever want to be a pirate, my hearty?"

Now John had often dreamed of joining a pirate ship, sailing the seven seas and making

Tick-tock! Tick-tock! Tick-tock!

"Didn't you ever want to be a pirate?"

people walk the plank. He quite liked the idea of Hook's invitation to become one.

"Perhaps I could call myself Red-handed Jack," he suggested.

"And a good name too," said Hook. "We'll call you that if you join us."

"What would you call me if I joined?" asked Michael.

"Blackbeard Joe," said Hook.

Michael was impressed. "What do you think, John?" he asked. "Shall we become pirates?"

John wasn't sure. First, he had a question for Hook. "Shall we still be the King's subjects?"

Hook sneered cruelly. "No, my little land-lubbers," he said, "you would have to swear a special oath: 'Down with the King'."

That was it as far as John was concerned. "Then I refuse," he said firmly. "I wish to remain a subject of the King."

"And I refuse too," shouted little Michael.

Hook was beside himself with anger. "That seals your fate," he bellowed. "Bring up the boys' mother! Prepare the plank!"

They were only young boys, and their faces went white when Cecco and Jukes brought out the dreaded plank.

Tick-tock! Tick-tock! Tick-tock!

Cecco and Jukes brought out the plank.

***

Wendy had been waiting anxiously down in the hold, all by herself. No words can describe how much she hated those pirates. To the boys, there was at least something glamorous about life as a pirate. But all Wendy saw was a filthy ship that had not been scrubbed for years.

There wasn't a floor or shelf that you couldn't scrawl your name on in the dust. Not one of the pirates ever cleaned or did the washing. No one bothered to wash up after supper.

Wendy was finally brought up on deck and taken to Hook.

"So, my beauty," said Hook, "you are here just in time to see your children walk the plank."

Fine gentlemen though he might have been, he still had a dirty mark on the collar of his white shirt. He saw that Wendy had spotted it. He tried to rub it away with a finger.

"Are all the boys to die?" asked Wendy, in a bold voice.

"They are," he roared, "but you now have the chance to have some final words with them. Silence men, for a mother's last words to her children!"

Wendy stepped forward proudly. "These are my last words, dear boys," she began. "I feel that I have a message to you from your real mothers, and it is this: 'We hope our sons will die like brave Englishmen'."

The pirates were impressed at Wendy's words, and they were even more amazed at Tootles's bravery.

"I will do as my mother wants," he cried. "What about you, Nibs?"

"The same," he said. "I shall die a brave Englishman. What say you, Twins?"

The Twins would have agreed, but Hook had lost his patience with all the talk of bravery and dying for England. "Tie Wendy up," he shouted, "so she can't fly away."

Smee tied her to the main mast of the ship. "Please, Wendy," he whispered as he played with the ropes, "I'll save you if you promise to be my mother."

But not even for Smee would she make such a promise. "Please tie me as tightly to the mast as you can," she ordered.

It was a sad thing to note that as Wendy was being tied up, not one of the boys was looking at her. The eyes of all were on the plank and that last little walk they were about to take.

121

Now, as the time approached, they had lost all hope. Their bravery was melting away and they began to shiver.

Hook smiled and moved toward Wendy. His intention was to turn her face away so that she would not have to witness her boys walking the plank one by one. But he never reached Wendy. He had heard something . . .

Tick-tock! Tick-tock! Tick-tock!

They all heard it; pirates, boys, and Wendy. Immediately every head turned, but not toward the sound.

Tying Wendy to the main mast of the ship.

Tick-tock! Tick-tock! Tick-tock!

They turned to look at Hook.

What a terrible change had come over him. It was as if someone had chopped his legs off. He had slumped into a helpless whimpering heap.

The sound came closer and closer. Everyone, including Hook, imagined that a crocodile must be about to board the ship. Hook started to crawl in the opposite direction to the noise. The pirates respectfully cleared a path for him.

"Hide me!" begged Hook.

The pirates pushed Hook into a cupboard and shut the door. Then they ran for their lives into the depths of the *Jolly Roger*. Meanwhile, the Lost Boys rushed to the side of the ship. They got the strangest surprise of their life. For it was no crocodile. It was Peter! He signaled to them not to give his presence away. Then he went on ticking.

Tick-tock! Tick-tock! Tick-tock!

Chapter 19
Cock-a-doodle-do

When we last saw Peter, he was stealing across the island with one finger to his lips and a dagger at the ready. He had seen the crocodile pass by him and noticed that it wasn't ticking any more. The clock must have stopped.

Peter wondered how he could turn the fact to his advantage. What he did was quite simple. He decided to use his skills of imitation by tick-tocking his way across the island. By sounding like the crocodile, all the other wild beasts would leave him alone.

Peter ticked wonderfully well. By the time he reached Kidd's Creek, he was still tick-tocking, and he had ticked so long now that he forgot to stop. The idea that his tick-tocking might frighten Hook hadn't even crossed his mind.

He had climbed up the side of the ship and was astonished to see the last of the pirates running for safety below decks shouting, "Crocodile! Crocodile!"

He had climbed up the side of the ship.

It was only then that Peter remembered he was still ticking. "How clever of me," he thought, as only Peter could. "How clever I am. No one else would have thought to frighten Hook by pretending to be the crocodile."

Peter even made a sign to the boys that there was no need to applaud him.

Just then, a pirate poked his head around a door to see what was happening. Peter gave him no chance; he quickly flew at the pirate and pushed him to the deck.

One of the boys cupped his hand over the pirate's mouth to keep him quiet. Four other boys caught him and threw him overboard. There was a splash and then silence.

"One!" cried Slightly, who had decided to count each pirate they overpowered, even if he wasn't sure whether there would be a second.

"Oh what a great game this all is," thought Peter, vanishing into Hook's cabin.

At that moment, some of the other pirates came out onto the deck again. Seeing no sign of the crocodile, they opened the cupboard where Hook was hiding.

"The crocodile's gone," said Smee.

"What crocodile?" asked Hook, pretending he had never had any worries about a crocodile.

126

"The crocodile's gone."

"I was just searching for something in this cupboard."

Hook emerged and saw the boys were still there, and Wendy was still tied to the mast.

"Right!" he said. "Now let's get on with this walking the plank. Are you ready boys? Perhaps you'd like a touch of the cat o' nine tails first."

"No! No!" cried the boys who knew only too well that the "cat" was a whip with nine vicious leather straps.

Hook just laughed. "Jukes," he said, "go and get the cat. It's in my cabin."

"Aye! Aye!" replied Jukes.

The cabin! Peter was in the cabin! The children gazed at each other, wondering what was going to happen next.

Hook now started to sing an old pirate song:

"Yo ho, yo ho, the frisky plank,
You walks along it so,
Till it goes down and you goes down,
To Davy Jones below!

Yo ho, yo ho, the scratching cat,
Its tails are nine, you know,
And when they write upon your back . . ."

128

What the last line was we'll never know. His singing stopped abruptly. A dreadful screech was heard coming from the captain's cabin. The sound wailed through the ship and died away. Then everyone heard a loud crowing sound. The children knew to whom that crow belonged.

"Two!" cried a delighted Slightly, knowing full well that Jukes had been overpowered by Peter.

"What was that?" shouted Hook.

The pirate Cecco plucked up his courage and advanced into the cabin, to see what was going on.

"What the matter?" asked Hook. "Where's Jukes?"

The voice of Cecco echoed from the dark cabin. "Bill Jukes has been knocked on the head and he's out like a light. That's what the matter is."

"Bill Jukes, knocked on the head!" cried the pirates as one.

"The cabin's as black as a pit," continued Cecco. "But there is something terrible in here that keeps on crowing."

The Lost Boys could hardly hide their smiles as Cecco emerged, running as if he'd been chased out by a ghost.

"Get back in there," ordered Hook. "And fetch me that cock-a-doodle-do!"

Chapter 20
Peter Pan the Avenger

The last thing that Cecco wanted to do was go back into Hook's cabin.

Hook grabbed his sword and poked Cecco in the ribs. "Are you going back, or do you want to die here?"

Cecco nervously entered the cabin again. A moment later there was a deathly scream and a thud, followed by the familiar crowing sound.

No one spoke except Slightly. "Three," he said quietly.

"Hell's teeth and odd fish," roared Hook. "Who will bring me that cock-a-doodle-do?"

Hook looked closely at his pirate dogs. "Did I hear you volunteer, Starkey?" he asked so politely.

"No, by thunder, I didn't," protested Starkey.

"By my hook, I think you did," smiled Hook.

"I'd rather walk the plank," cried Starkey, "before I go in there."

"Is this mutiny then?" asked Hook. "Get back into my cabin or the plank will be your end!"

There was nothing that could persuade Starkey to go into the cabin and meet whatever terrifying creature lurked within. With no more ado, he threw himself overboard.

"Four," muttered Slightly.

Smee quickly followed him.

"Five," said Slightly.

"Blast you all!" said Hook. "I'll go in myself. I'll bring out that infernal cock-a-doodle-do."

Hook lit a candle and, sword in hand, entered the cabin.

Slightly was preparing to shout "six" when Hook came out again. "Something blew out my candle!" he announced rather nervously.

"Something?" echoed Mullins.

"What of Cecco?" asked Noodler.

"He seems to have disappeared and so has Jukes," muttered Hook.

Now Hook had an idea. He turned to the remaining pirates and told them to drive all the Lost Boys into the cabin. "Let them fight the cock-a-doodle-do," he said. "If they kill it, well and good. If they die, well, I was going to kill the boys anyway."

He threw himself overboard.

This was an order that Hook's men were delighted to follow. Equally, it was an idea that the Lost Boys were delighted to play along with. Oh, how they pretended to be frightened as the chains around their feet were removed before they were pushed into the cabin and the door was slammed shut behind them.

"Now listen!" said Hook.

All the pirates listened and waited, but none were brave enough to face the cabin door.

The only person to look at the door was Wendy, who was still tied to the mast.

She was not waiting for a scream or a crow. She was waiting for the reappearance of Peter ... and she hadn't long to wait.

In the cabin, the boys found their leader, Peter Pan. They also found Jukes and Cecco. Peter had bound and gagged the villains, and pushed them behind some sacks of pirate treasure. There was no need to worry about them for the moment.

Neither Hook, nor his men saw what happened next. They still couldn't bring themselves to look toward the cabin. If they had, they would have seen Peter and the other boys emerge.

The first thing Peter did was free Wendy from the mast. Then he took in a great breath

In the cabin, the boys found their leader.

and crowed as loud as he could. To the pirates, it was a voice saying that the thing in the cabin had killed all the boys. They were panic stricken. Hook tried to hearten them, but he was almost as terrified as they were.

"I know!" said Flint. "It's the girl that's been causing all this business. It's bad luck to have a girl aboard. We'll be alright when she's gone. Fling the girl overboard this minute."

The pirates were prepared to risk anything now. They turned around, only to see that Wendy was no longer tied to the mast.

"What now!" cried Hook.

"She's gone!" wailed the remaining pirates together.

"I can see she's gone!" roared Hook. "But where?"

Hook and the pirates were staring blankly at the place where Wendy had been tied, when a small figure came out of the dark shadows.

"Who's that?" said Hook. "He looks familiar."

"It's Peter Pan the avenger!' was the terrible answer.

Suddenly, Hook and every pirate knew exactly who the cock-a-doodle-do was!

Chapter 21
The Final Battle

Captain Hook looked up at Peter Pan, who was crowing like a mad thing.

"Get him, you dogs!" he cried to his fellow pirates.

Peter was ready. "Down boys and at 'em!" he crowed.

Had the pirates kept together, it is certain they would have had the advantage in the coming battle. Man for man they were stronger, but they were spread all over the ship. This helped Peter and the boys to hunt down the enemy in pairs, choosing their quarry at will.

Some pirates remained hidden below decks. They weren't safe either. Slightly wasn't a fighter, but he went all over the ship with his lantern. Each time he found a pirate, he flashed it in their face. The terrified half-blinded pirates ran for their lives.

There was little sound to be heard apart

from the clang of weapons, an occasional screech or splash, and Slightly calling out the tally of pirates who were dead, or who had jumped overboard:

"Six, seven, eight, nine, ten, eleven . . ."

By now Peter's boys had got rid of most of Hook's men. They'd even dragged the unfortunate Jukes and Cecco from the cabin, untied them, and thrown them overboard. Yet somehow, the captain was single-handedly still keeping all his attackers at bay. Again and again they closed on him but like a dancer, he always found an escape route to fight again.

When the captain was really in trouble, he lifted up an occasional boy or two with his hook. Tootles and John were both dangling from that hook when Peter Pan came to their rescue with a sword in his hand.

"Put down your weapons, boys," he cried, "and leave Hook to me. It's him or me now!"

Hook flicked his hook and sent Tootles and John flying. Now, at last, he found himself face-to-face with Peter. The others drew back and formed a circle around the two sworn enemies.

For a long time, the two just looked at each other. Hook was shaking a little but Peter had a strange, cocky, smile on his face.

Keeping his attackers at bay

"So Pan," said Hook at last. "This is all your doing, is it?"

"Aye, it is, Captain James Hook," replied Peter boldly. "A ticking crocodile, a crowing cock-a-doodle-do. It's all my doing."

"Proud and cocky youth," said Hook, "prepare to meet your end."

Without further ado, the fight began.

Peter was a superb swordsman, darting to and fro, parrying and lunging with dazzling speed. Yet Hook was his match, turning and circling like a man possessed. Whenever Peter was about to make a fatal strike, Hook darted out of reach. And when Peter did get in close, Hook often used his other weapon. The iron hook was just as dangerous.

Time and time again, Peter had to duck down to save himself. Hook's sword came swishing over, quickly followed by the flying hook. The onlookers expected Hook to strike Peter at any moment. But Peter watched and learned. He was ready when Hook tried the trick again.

Across came the sword at a terrible speed. Peter ducked as it almost separated his head from his shoulders. Next came the hook. As soon as it had flown past, Peter thrust out his sword. It pierced Hook in the ribs.

Hook stood frozen in shock for a moment as he saw the blood begin to trickle.

He could never stand the sight of his own blood. His sword slipped from his hand and clanged to the ground.

The pirate captain was at Peter's mercy.

"Now!" shouted all the boys. "Hook is ours!"

But Peter would have none of it. He knew how frightened Hook was of seeing his own

Across came the sword at terrible speed.

blood and thought it was an unfair way to finish the fight. So he picked up Hook's sword and gave it back to him. "The fight is not over yet," he said. "I'll give you another chance."

Up until that moment, Hook had seen Peter Pan as simply a mysterious boy who was determined to kill him. But now he wasn't so sure.

"Pan," he asked, "who or what are you?"

"I'm youth. I'm joy. I'm mischief!" Peter crowed. "I'm a little bird that has just broken out of its egg."

He was, of course, talking nonsense. It was proof to Hook that Peter didn't know who or what he was. That only frightened the pirate more. He was sure Pan belonged to another planet.

"On guard!" Hook cried, his sword flashing through the air.

Now it was Peter's turn to dart backward and forward, taunting Hook to keep attacking him. It was too much for Hook. He was becoming exhausted. At last he threw down his sword and ran to one of the ship's gunpowder barrels.

Hook grabbed one of the ship's lanterns and threw it in. "You have a minute," he said, "before the barrel explodes. And that'll sink the ship and all aboard her."

Peter didn't hesitate. He lunged forward, put his shoulder to the barrel, and heaved it overboard.

Hook was done for. Now all the boys were running around him, taunting him. He could not have cared less; his mind was a million miles away.

He was back at his famous school, playing football. It was a game where the opposition had lost because he had cheated by tripping up a player who was just about to score the winning goal. He had saved the game for his side but at what cost. He had disgraced his side by cheating.

Now, so many years on, poor Hook decided to at last make amends. He would cheat and lie no longer. He would face defeat gracefully this time and nobly, too. He would throw himself into the sea.

"Pan!" he shouted, clambering onto the side of the ship. "Sadly, I must leave you now. Farewell."

Peter thought he was trying to escape once again. He rushed across and struck him with his sword.

"That was not the act of a gentleman," said Hook, now teetering on the side of the ship. "I was going to throw myself in."

The Final Battle

"Sadly, I must leave you now."

At last, Hook tumbled over the side. The last words that Peter heard Hook say were: "Pan, you're no gentleman."

That hurt Peter—but not as much as Hook was about to be hurt as he tumbled toward the sea. Just as he neared the surface, a silent creature rose from the deep and opened its jaws. It was the crocodile! Hook vanished inside. The crocodile ate him with one swallow, closed its jaws, and swam away without so much as a tick or a tock.

"Seventeen!" shouted Slightly.

Chapter 22
Captain Peter Pan

Slightly's arithmetic wasn't perfect. Fifteen pirates paid the penalty for their pirating crimes that night, and ended up in the sea. They all decided to give up being pirates and joined the Indians instead.

Wendy had watched the fight from near the mast. She was so proud of how Peter and the boys had fought. But she was horrified when she caught sight of the clock in the captain's cabin. It was one o'clock in the morning!

"To bed with you all," she insisted. "It's far too late for you to still be up."

She did get all but one of them to bed in the pirates' bunks. It had been an exhausting night and they soon fell asleep.

Peter refused to do as Wendy said. He continued to strut up and down the deck as if he was on guard. Finally, he fell asleep across one of the ship's cannons. Wendy went out and took him back to a bunk in the captain's cabin.

At dawn the next day, everyone was up early. The night before had been so exciting. Now all the Lost Boys were playing at being real pirates.

There was a stormy sea and the *Jolly Roger* was tossing and turning in the giant waves. Tootles was up front, pulling on sail ropes as hard as he could. He had dressed specially that morning. He was in pirate's trousers, cut off at the knees. He kept hitching up his trousers with a wonderful nautical roll.

Down below decks, other members of the crew were arguing about what sort of ship it should be. Most thought it best that the *Jolly Roger* remained a pirate ship. Some did think it should be a more honest ship. But there was only one person who had the power to decide what sort of ship it was going to be. That was the captain.

It will come as no surprise to anyone to find Captain Peter Pan at the wheel with Nibs and John his most senior officers. And Peter definitely wanted it to be a pirate ship. As far as he was concerned, anyone who argued with him could walk the plank.

The general view was that Peter was a good captain for the time being. But it was anybody's

Finally, he fell asleep.

guess what would happen when Wendy had finished making him a new suit from one of Captain Hook's old uniforms.

You can guess what happened on the night that he first wore the suit. He sat in the captain's cabin yelling "Brimstone and gall" every few minutes, and imagining that he had an iron hook for a right arm.

Later, he called all the crew together and told them that they were all pirate dogs. "So don't you think of mutiny!" he shouted. "I'll slap you all in irons if you do."

Peter was enjoying himself. So were the others. They liked the way Captain Peter talked. It was good seafaring language and they cheered him wildly.

Peter gave a few more orders and then turned the ship toward the mainland once more. He had calculated that if the good weather lasted, they should strike the tropical Azores Islands by the middle of June.

Why the Azores? Peter guessed that once they reached there, it would be quicker for Wendy, John, Michael, and the others to fly the rest of the way to No. 14.

"Raise all sail," cried Captain Peter. "Full speed ahead!"

Captain Peter Pan at the wheel.

Chapter 23
Sadness at No. 14

Now we must return to the nursery at No. 14.
We are merely traveling ahead of the children
to see that their beds are made up properly.

We must also be sure that the Darlings are
not going out for the night. It would certainly
spoil the surprise that Wendy, John, and
Michael were planning to give their parents on
Thursday week, which is when they were due
to return. Each moment on the ship, they had
been imagining their mother's delight and
father's joy at seeing them home again.

They need not have worried.

Mrs. Darling had not left the house since her
children had vanished with Peter Pan. All the
beds had been aired and made up, and each day,
she checked that the nursery window was left
open. The only change to be seen in the nursery
was that Nana was sleeping there once more.

As for Mr. Darling, he'd felt so guilty about
what had happened on the night he chained

Nana in the yard. He blamed himself for the children flying away. He now accepted that Nana was far wiser than him, and he punished himself by going to live in the yard, in Nana's kennel.

Mrs. Darling begged Mr. Darling to come into the house but he just wouldn't. He said he would stay there until the children returned. He still had to go to the city to work, so each morning the kennel was carried—with Mr. Darling in it—to the taxi which took him to his office. He always politely lifted his bowler hat to anyone who peered inside the kennel.

When the story of why Mr. Darling now lived in a kennel got out, he became quite famous. Crowds would follow his cab every morning and when his important friends asked him out to dinner, they always said, "Oh, do bring your kennel."

***

On the evening of the Thursday week Mrs. Darling was sitting in the nursery with Nana, awaiting her husband's return. The fire was burning in the grate and all was cozy and warm.

Mrs. Darling now looked a very sad mother. All the happiness in her life had long since vanished. That little mysterious kiss hidden on the corner of her mouth had almost disappeared. Tears often rolled down her face, especially when she was asleep.

Mr. Darling was late home that night and she dozed off in front of the fire. Shall we slip a message into Mrs. Darling's sleeping head to tell her that the children are now just two miles away and flying strong? Yes, let's.

Oh dear. It's a pity we did. She woke up and started to call out the children's names!

"Oh Nana," she said. "I dreamed that the children were on their way back."

Mr. Darling returned soon after. He and his kennel were brought up to the nursery. He was so tired that he fell asleep immediately. Mrs. Darling fell into another deep sleep, too.

That was the moment that two figures flew in through the nursery window.

Two figures, I hear you say. But there were three children who left the nursery to fly to Neverland! The truth was that the two figures were Peter and Tinker Bell.

Peter's first words revealed everything.

"Quick, Tink," he said. "Close the window!

Mr. Darling went to live in Nana's kennel.

Bar it! Then when Wendy gets here she'll find it locked. She'll think her parents don't want to see her ever again."

How Peter danced with glee at his cruel plan. He would do anything to keep Wendy for himself, in Neverland. Suddenly, he spotted Mrs. Darling asleep in the chair. "You'll never see Wendy, John, or Michael ever again," he said.

Then he saw the tears on Mrs. Darling's face.

Peter shut his eyes. He found it hard to look at the tears. When he opened his eyes again, he saw that two more tears had rolled out of Mrs. Darling's sleeping eyes.

"I am sorry," he said at last. "I love Wendy as much as you, but we can't both have her."

Now, it was almost as if the sleeping Mrs. Darling was talking in Peter's head. "Please let me have my dear children back," she said. "I shall die of sadness if they never return."

It was all too much for Peter. He skipped about and made funny faces. He started singing. But nothing could take his mind off the sleeping Mrs. Darling. "Alright," he said, angrily. "Who needs a silly mother anyway? Come on Tink. We're going back to Neverland.

"Quick Tink, close the window!"

But remember to leave the nursery window open."

So Peter and Tinker Bell flew out of the window and up into the stars . . .

Chapter 24
Home at Last

A short time after Peter and Tinker Bell had left the nursery, Wendy, John, and Michael flew in through the open window. They alighted on the floor. Poor Michael was so young when he left for Neverland, that he couldn't remember the nursery at all.

"I say," said John. "There's a man sleeping in Nana's kennel!"

"It's father!" said an astonished Wendy.

"Let me see," begged Michael, who thought it was a very strange thing indeed for a man to sleep in a kennel.

"Surely," said John, "he didn't sleep in there before."

"John," said Wendy, a little confused, "perhaps we don't remember what the old life was like as well as we thought we did."

Now they saw Mrs. Darling asleep in front of the fire.

"Let's all slip back into our beds," she said.

"Then in the morning mother will find us all, as if we'd never been away."

So that's what they did. They undressed and went to bed. It had been such an exhausting day, with such a lot of flying, that they were asleep in moments.

The next morning the children were awake early, hoping to see how surprised mother would be. Mrs. Darling, who had slept in the chair all night, did wake up. And she did see the children in their beds.

"There's a man sleeping in Nana's kennel!"

The children waited for her cry of joy, but it never came. You see, she had seen them in their beds so often in her dreams that she thought it was just another dream.

Now a cold fear came over the children. Had mother forgotten them? Was she so angry that she would never speak to them again?

"Mother!" cried Wendy.

"That sounds like Wendy," said Mrs. Darling, but she was still sure it was a dream.

"Mother!" cried John.

"That's John's voice," she said.

"Mother!" cried Michael.

"That's Michael," she said, stretching out her arms as if to welcome the three children who would never return.

But they had returned. And now they all got out of bed and tiptoed across until they all fitted into her arms. At last, Mrs. Darling realized it was not a dream. She burst into tears and hugged all three as never before.

"I fought some pirates, Mummy," said Michael.

"I did, too," said John.

"I saw mermaids," said Wendy. "And Peter Pan and the Lost Boys built me a house."

"We lived underground mostly," said John.

She hugged all three as never before.

Mrs. Darling, with tears of joy pouring down her face, could not get a word in edgeways. Her children wanted to tell her everything.

"A crocodile ate Hook," said Michael.

"And I got shot by an arrow because of a fairy!" cried Wendy.

"I was first officer on the *Jolly Roger*," said John.

How much Mrs. Darling believed is another matter.

The excited children woke up Nana and Mr. Darling. There never was a happier sight than the Darling family together again.

There was only one other witness there to see the happy scene. Peter was now sitting on the window sill looking into the room. He had such a sad look on his face. He knew the love and warmth shared by a family was one joy that he would never know.

Chapter 25
The Lost Boys Get a Mother

And what of the Lost Boys? Where were Tootles, Nibs, Slightly, Curly, and the Twins?

They had flown to the Darling's home with Peter and Tink but out of politeness, they had stayed outside the house. They thought it would be kinder to let Wendy, John, and Michael give their mother a surprise first.

When they did go in, they didn't fly in by the window. They went in by the front door and up the stairs. They thought it would make a better impression. Now they stood in a row in front of Mrs. Darling, with their hats off. They rather wished they weren't still wearing their pirates' clothes.

They did not say a word, but the message from their eyes was unmistakable: "Please can we stay with you?"

Of course, Mrs. Darling said at once that they could stay.

Mr. Darling wasn't so sure. "There are

They stood in a row in front of Mrs. Darling.

rather a lot of you," he said.

"If you think we'll be too much trouble," said one of the Twins, "perhaps we should go."

"Father!" cried Wendy. "You couldn't send them away!"

"We could lie four to a bed," said Nibs.

"And I could cut their hair," said Wendy.

Then Mr. Darling burst into tears. In truth, he was as glad as Mrs. Darling to see them. "Come with me," he sniffed. "I'll show you the house."

The Lost Boys were so excited that they danced after him.

As for Peter, he saw Wendy once more before he flew away.

"Hello," he said, flying back through the window and landing at her feet. "Goodbye."

"Oh dear," said Wendy, "are you going away?"

"Yes," he replied.

At that moment, Mrs. Darling came across, no doubt keeping an eye on him to make sure he didn't fly off with Wendy again. "I have adopted all the other boys," she said. "I can adopt you too if you want."

"Would you send me to school?" asked Peter.

"Yes," said Mrs. Darling.

"And into an office to work when I get older?" asked Peter.

"I suppose so," she replied.

"And will I become a grown-up?"

"Oh, very soon," laughed Mrs. Darling.

"Ugh!" said Peter. "I don't want to go to school to learn silly things. I could never work in an office. And I never want to grow up. If I was to wake up one day and find I was growing a beard, I wouldn't know what I would do."

Mrs. Darling felt so sorry for Peter, and she reached out to hug him.

"Keep back," he cried. "No one is going to catch me and make me go to school."

"But where are you going to live?" asked Mrs. Darling.

"With Tink in the little house we built for Wendy," he said. "The fairies will put it on top of a tree for us."

"Oh, are there still fairies?" asked Mrs. Darling. "I thought they were all dead."

"Oh no," said Wendy, who now considered herself an expert on the subject. "When a new baby laughs for the first time, a new fairy is born."

"I shall have such fun with Tink in our own little Wendy House," said Peter.

She reached out to hug him.

166

"It might be rather lonely in the evening," suggested Wendy.

"Never," said Peter. "The Indians will come and dance for us at night. The mermaids will sing for us, too. We shall be very jolly."

"Oh, mother," sighed Wendy. "I would love to live in the Wendy House."

"Wendy, you could still be our mother," said Peter.

"But Wendy needs a mother too," said Mrs. Darling. "She is still so very young."

'What if," said Peter, "what if Wendy comes for a week every year to do the spring cleaning?"

"We shall have to see," said Mrs. Darling.

"Well, we must be gone," said Peter.

"Don't forget me," said Wendy, knowing how short Peter's memory was. "Try to remember me until springtime."

"Of course I will," said Peter, swooping down and flying past Mrs. Darling's mouth.

In that instant, he stole that single kiss that no one else had ever managed to win. Then he was gone. He flew high into the sky with the familiar twinkling light of Tinker Bell beside him.

Chapter 26
When Wendy Grew Up

Life at No. 14 settled down after that. The children went back to school. At night, Nana tied their feet together to make sure they didn't fly away.

As time passed, the children's memories started to fade a little. Michael still believed in the magic of Neverland, but Wendy and John were starting to wonder if their Neverland adventures had ever happened. However, Peter did arrive the following spring, and he and Wendy flew off to Neverland once more.

Wendy had so looked forward to talking about her memories of Neverland, but new adventures had crowded the old ones from Peter's memory.

"Who is Captain Hook?" he asked one night.

"Don't you remember?" said Wendy. "You chased him into the crocodile's jaws and saved all our lives."

"Oh, I forget people all the time," said Peter.

And when Wendy asked to see Tinker Bell, Peter was puzzled.

"Who is Tinker Bell?" he asked.

Wendy did spring clean the Wendy House for Peter that year. But the following year, he did not come for her. "Perhaps he is ill," Wendy said to John.

"You know Peter is never ill," said John.

Peter did remember to collect Wendy for spring-cleaning the following year. The strange thing was that he never knew he had missed a year.

That was the last time Wendy saw him, as a young girl. She did try to keep Peter alive in her mind as she started to grow up, but now the years came and went without any sign of him. John and Michael had grown up too. Michael became an engine driver. John was a doctor.

These days you will see the Lost Boys going to work in a taxi. They each carry a little leather bag and an umbrella, in case it rains. Tootles became a judge and Slightly married a judge's daughter.

Wendy was married too, and had a daughter called Jane. Of course, Wendy told her daughter stories of Peter Pan and Tinker Bell, and the Lost Boys. How Jane loved those stories, especially the ones about flying to Neverland!

Wendy's nursery was now Jane's nursery. There were two beds in the nursery now, Jane's and her nurse's. There was no kennel. Lovely Nana had passed away a long time ago.

Once a week, Jane's nurse had the night off. Then it was Wendy's job to put her to bed. As she was going to bed, Jane asked Wendy a question.

"Did you fly when you were very little?"

"I think I did," replied Wendy, "but I sometimes wonder if I really did."

"Why don't you fly now?"

"Because I'm a grown-up," said Wendy. "When people grow up, they forget. But I do remember the night Peter lost his shadow and I sewed it on for him. Soon after that, we all flew off to Neverland."

"And which bits of Neverland did you like best?" asked Jane.

Wendy gave a long list. "The fairies, pirates, Indians, and mermaids. But I think I liked the home under the ground best of all. Of course, I loved Peter like a son. He was such a cocky little boy though—you should have heard him crowing!"

170

The following year, he did not come for her.

"What did his crow sound like?" asked Jane.

"It went like this," said Wendy, trying to imitate Peter's crow.

"No it didn't," said Jane. "It went like this."

Jane then gave a perfect imitation of Peter's crow.

Wendy was startled. "My darling, how could you know how Peter crows?"

"I often hear it when I'm sleeping," said Jane.

"Ah yes," said Wendy. "Many children hear it when they are sleeping. I was the one of the few who heard it when I was awake."

"Lucky you," said Jane.

Wendy sat in the nursery chair and dozed, while Jane fell asleep. Suddenly, the nursery window blew open. Wendy awoke with a start as a cold evening breeze blew into the room. Then Peter dropped down onto the floor, looking exactly the same as before. Wendy saw that he was still a little boy.

"Hello, Wendy," he said.

"Hello, Peter," she answered, pinching herself to make sure she was awake and he was real.

"You have grown up," he said. "You promised that you'd never grow up."

"I couldn't help it," she said. "I have a little daughter of my own now."

Now, the little imp in Peter's character woke up. "You have a little daughter?" he said.

"Yes," replied Wendy. "Her name is Jane. She is sleeping."

Without another word, Peter flew across to Jane's bedside and looked at the little creature. "Hello, Jane," he said.

Jane woke up and saw the delightful little boy beside her. "Who are you?" she asked.

"I'm Peter Pan," he replied. "I live in Neverland; second to the right and straight on till morning."

Poor Wendy! It was the same conversation that she'd had with Peter so many years earlier. She knew exactly what he would ask next.

"Can you fly?" he asked.

"No," said Jane.

"Then I will teach you" said Peter.

"Oh, how lovely," said Jane.

"I'll teach you to climb on the wind's back," he said, "and then away we'll go."

Wendy knew there was nothing she could do. She knew that Peter would teach Jane to fly. She knew that Peter would fly away with her to Neverland.

Watching Peter and Jane flying around the stars

When Wendy Grew Up

Of course, Wendy let them fly away together in the end. Our last glimpse of Wendy shows her at the nursery window, watching Peter and Jane flying around the stars.

***

That all happened a very long time ago. Jane is now a grown-up and has a daughter called Margaret. Peter Pan came and taught her to fly and then flew with her to Neverland, too. There, she told him stories about Captain Hook, mermaids, and Indians. He had forgotten all about them.

When Margaret grows up, she too will have a daughter. And like Wendy, Jane, and Margaret before her, she too will be mother to the boy who never grew up.

And so it will go on for generation after generation—until children lose their innocence and don't believe in fairies any more.

The End